WILD CHILD

Forest's First Home

Tara Zann

[Imprint]
MAKE YOUR MARK

New York

[Imprint]
MAKE YOUR MARK

A part of Macmillan Children's Publishing Group,
a division of Macmillan Publishing Group, LLC

WILD CHILD: FOREST'S FIRST HOME. Copyright © 2017 by Imprint.
All rights reserved. Printed in the United States of America by
LSC Communications, Harrisonburg, Virginia.
For information, address
Imprint, 175 Fifth Avenue, New York, N.Y. 10010.

Library of Congress Cataloging-in-Publication Data is available.
ISBN 978-1-250-10383-3 (paperback) /
ISBN 978-1-250-10382-6 (ebook)

Our books may be purchased in bulk for promotional,
educational, or business use. Please contact your local
bookseller or the Macmillan Corporate and Premium Sales
Department at (800) 221-7945 ext. 5442 or by e-mail at
MacmillanSpecialMarkets@macmillan.com.

Book design by Ellen Duda
Illustrations by Dan Widdowson
Imprint logo designed by Amanda Spielman

First Edition—2017

2 4 6 8 10 9 7 5 3 1

mackids.com

This book is guarded by a child
who grew up to be quite wild.
Beware stealing this book, you crook,
as down on a vine this child will swing
to knock you over and steal back this lost thing.

For wild children everywhere

Chapter 1

Early one morning, Olive Regle woke up in time to see the sun rise. She climbed out of the tent at her family's campsite and smiled as she heard the birds whistling one another awake. She bundled up, sat down on a camping chair, and waited for her father to wake.

For some reason, Olive felt like it was taking her father *forever*, but really it had

been only about fifteen minutes. Then she heard:

"Argh!"

Olive laughed to herself, realizing their dog, Bailey, had woken up her father with lots of sloppy kisses. She knew there was no way he was getting back to sleep now.

"All right! All right!" Olive heard her

father say to Bailey. "Just don't wake up Ryan."

"Too late," grumbled Ryan, Olive's ten-year-old brother.

"Good morning, Olive," said her dad as he came out of the tent. "Hot chocolate?"

"Yes, please!" said Olive.

"I'll boil the water," he said.

"I'll get the marshmallows," said Olive. They had had the same exact conversation the past three mornings.

As she looked around, Olive realized they were the first ones up in the entire campground. But that was fine with her. School started in a few days, and Olive was happy to spend some time with her dad. He worked a lot, and Olive wished he didn't. They both loved to be outdoors, and this camping trip had been Olive's favorite part of the summer so far.

Ryan emerged from the tent, groggy and grumpy. He took a cup of hot chocolate and sat down in one of their camping chairs. Unlike Olive, Ryan was *not* a morning person. He was barely an afternoon person.

"Dad, I was thinking that—" began Olive.

"Dad, can I have some more marshmallows?" interrupted Ryan.

"Sure," their dad replied, handing him some.

Olive tried again. "I was hoping that—"

"When are we leaving?" Ryan interrupted her again.

Olive pouted. Sometimes her brother

was okay, but sometimes he was down-right annoying.

"Dad,canItakeBaileyforawalk?" Olive said, super fast so Ryan couldn't interrupt her.

Her father looked up from his mug of instant coffee. "That's a good idea before we get back in the car. Don't go too far, though. While you're gone, Ryan and I can pack up the tent and gear."

"Wait! What?" began Ryan, launching into a tirade about the unfairness of life in general, and especially the unfairness of who was packing the car.

Olive saw her opportunity and quickly grabbed Bailey's leash, scampering off with a hidden smile. "Come on, boy," she said to the golden retriever. She attached his leash and they headed away from the campsite.

The pair walked down a well-worn trail. Olive could hear birds calling to one another overhead. She often wondered what they were saying. Meanwhile, Bailey was on high alert for any sudden movement or strange smell—from a squirrel, skunk, or other woodland creature. While Bailey kept his head down, Olive looked at the trees towering above. The trees

were taller and wider than any building Olive had ever seen. She imagined them being part of a sprawling kingdom, complete with enchanted creatures.

At that moment, Bailey barked and pulled sharply on his leash. Before she knew what was happening, the leash slipped out of Olive's hand.

"Bailey! Bailey!" yelled Olive. "Come back here!"

But the dog had spotted a squirrel and was determined to catch it. He ran off the trail and into the lush green woods.

Olive had no choice but to follow. She ran as fast as her eight-year-old legs would carry her, calling out Bailey's name. On her right, she heard a rustling in a bush.

"Bailey?" she called hesitantly.

The noise turned out to be just a

squirrel. She watched as it hopped from the bush to the trunk of the gigantic tree next to it. Soon another squirrel joined the first one, and the two looked like they were playing a game of tag.

Olive kept walking and calling for her dog. She heard more rustling up ahead and ran to it, hoping it was Bailey. She carefully walked toward the sound, dead leaves crunching under her shoes. She held her breath, pulled back a leafy branch, and gasped.

It wasn't Bailey. It was someone else entirely.

Chapter 2

Right in front of Olive was a boy who looked about her age. He was covered in a layer of dirt and was wearing a shirt and a pair of shorts that looked to be made of leaves, mud, and who knows what else. His hair was messy and ragged, and appeared to have parts of an actual bird's nest in it. His green eyes shone wide and curious. Before Olive could say anything,

the boy scampered up the closest tree and onto a high branch.

"Wait!" called Olive.

The boy stopped and peered down at her. Olive looked up. She smiled. He smiled back. A tiny bird poked its head out of the boy's hair, let loose an irritated chirp, and flew off.

"Please come back," she said shyly.

Rather than climb down, the boy grasped a vine and swung through the air.

Olive gasped as he let go, flipped backward, and landed perfectly in front of her. *Who is this boy?* Olive had never seen anything like his acrobatics! Speechless, Olive began to clap. The boy seemed surprised by this but immediately started to clap, too.

"I'm Olive," she said, pointing to herself. "What's your name?"

"Forest," replied the boy.

"Yes, this is a forest," said Olive. "But what's your name?"

"Forest," the boy replied.

"Your *name* is Forest?" she asked.

Forest nodded.

"Oh," said Olive. "I like that name."

Forest grinned. "Me too."

Suddenly, Forest dove toward Olive's feet and used a stick to help him yank up a three-foot rattlesnake.

Olive gasped. "Wow! I didn't even see it down there! What a giant snake! Is it a dangerous one?"

Forest nodded. "Rattlesnakes can be."

"Thank you for saving me," Olive said shyly but meaningfully.

Forest shrugged. "No problem." He put the snake down, and they watched it slither away.

"Where is your campsite?" asked Olive. "Ours is over there. My family is packing everything up. Do you want to come meet them?"

Forest looked sad suddenly. "No family. Just Forest."

Olive looked confused. "You don't have any parents? But . . . but . . . where do you live?"

Forest gestured to the wide expanse of woods around them. "This how Forest lives." Then he smiled deviously. "Forest watches all the campers. Forest learn many words from them: *diaper, pesky bugs,*

bathroom stinks, poison oak, dead battery, frozen hot dogs, and *you kids enjoy nature.*"

"That sounds like campers, all right," said Olive.

"But Forest has question," he said.

"Yes?" replied Olive.

"What is an Xbox?"

Olive giggled.

Just then, they heard a bark, and Olive turned to see Bailey running up to them.

"There you are!" she said.

Before she could grab his leash, Bailey started barking wildly at Forest.

"Stop, Bailey!" insisted Olive. "This is Forest. He's . . . my new friend."

At that, Forest smiled.

Bailey calmed down, and Olive rubbed

behind his ears, making his tongue hang out happily.

Forest knelt down to Bailey's eye level. The dog barked.

"Bailey says he *had* to chase the squirrel," said Forest.

"How do you know that's what he said?" asked Olive, not quite believing the boy.

"You don't?" asked Forest.

"No! Of course not!" said Olive.

"Huh," said Forest with a shrug. "Guess Forest just good with animals."

"Okay," Olive said, a bit suspicious. Then she suddenly felt shy and looked down at her shoes. "Um . . . do you want to come meet my family? They're just over this way." She turned to point in the direction she'd come from. When she turned back, Forest was gone.

"Forest? Forest?" called Olive. But there was no reply. Her shoulders sank and she frowned, feeling disappointed. She kind of liked having someone to talk to who didn't interrupt her all the time.

She looked down at Bailey. "Well, I guess we'd better head back before Dad starts to wonder what's taking us so long," she said. She and the dog turned back toward the campsite. On the way there, Olive's head was filled with questions about Forest: *Where does he sleep? What does he eat? Does he get lonely? Does he ever brush his teeth?*

Olive let Bailey lead the way back, hoping he was sniffing out their campsite instead of more squirrels. Before long, Bailey barked at the sight of Ryan and their father putting food back into the cooler.

Olive ran the last few yards, eager to share what had happened.

"Dad! Ryan!" she called. "You're not going to believe what happened to me!"

"Honey, there's a storm rolling in," said her father. "Can you tell us in the car?"

Olive looked up at the sky, and sure

enough, dark clouds were swirling in the distance.

"But I met this boy who lives in the woods! He can climb trees and swing through the air on vines and—"

Ryan snickered. "Can he find the magic pot of gold at the end of the rainbow, too?"

Olive shot him a nasty look. "I'm *not* making this up."

Her dad piped up. "I'm sure you're not. But if we don't get packed up lickety-split, I'm also *sure* we're going to be caught in the middle of this storm!"

"Yeah," said Ryan. "You heard Dad. We don't have time!"

Olive stuck her tongue out at her brother. Then they all raced around to pack away the gear and load up the car.

As soon as the first drop of rain fell, the gray clouds seemed to open up and empty out all their water. Olive and her family got soaked as they shoved the last few things into the car and then ducked inside themselves.

Once they were buckled in and driving away from the campsite, Olive looked out the smeary window, watching the

raindrops slide down the glass. Through the gray mist, she tried to spot Forest in the trees above but had no luck.

"It wasn't a dream," Olive said quietly to herself. "It was real, right, Bailey? You saw him, didn't you?"

Bailey, who was in the rear area of the car behind a pet barrier, didn't respond. Instead Olive heard the dog's gentle snores. She sighed.

After the long drive home, the rain cleared and everyone was thrilled to finally get out of the car. Olive was happy to see their blue house with its white shutters. Olive's father opened the garage door to unload the gear. Ryan tried to duck inside.

"Not so fast," his father said. "Help us unload."

"Aw, man!" grumbled Ryan.

Meanwhile, Olive went to the back of the car to let Bailey out. When she swung open the door, she was shocked. Sleeping right next to Bailey was none other than Forest!

Chapter 3

At the sound of the car door opening, Bailey yawned and shook himself out. Forest did the same.

"What are you doing here?" Olive sputtered. She couldn't believe Forest had been in the car the entire drive back! She didn't know what to do. Should she hide Forest? Should she introduce him? Would her father be mad? Would Ryan believe her now?

The decision was made for her as Bailey jumped out of the car and Forest followed.

"Wait!" called Olive.

But it was too late. Her brother had seen Forest. Ryan looked at the dirty and grubby boy, then at Olive, very, very confused.

"Who is this?" her dad asked, coming up to them.

She gazed over at Forest, but he was already hanging upside down from the house's rain gutter. Olive laughed nervously. "Uh . . . it's a funny story. You won't believe it, actually."

"Is he a friend of yours from school?" asked her father.

"Uh . . . no."

"Is he a new neighbor?" he asked.

"Uh . . . not exactly," she said.

"Where is he from, then?" asked her dad.

"He's from the back of the car . . . ?" Olive offered quietly as her voice dwindled to a whisper.

Her dad gave her a look.

"Well, I *tried* to tell you I saw a boy in the woods, but *someone* didn't believe me." She glared at Ryan.

"Don't drag me into this!" said Ryan.

"I didn't think you'd bring him home with us!" said her father.

"I didn't! He must have snuck into the car while we were packing up!"

Curious what all the talk was about, Forest climbed down and stood next to Olive. He smiled widely. He pointed to himself and said, "Forest."

Olive smiled at him. "Forest is my friend. He protected me from a dangerous rattlesnake."

"That's ridiculous," said Ryan.

"It's true!" insisted Olive. Before her brother could say another word, Olive turned to her father. "Can we keep him? I mean, can he stay?"

"Of course he can't stay!" sputtered Ryan.

Their father nodded. "I'm afraid Ryan's right. I'm sure, uh, *Forest* has a family wondering where he is right now."

Forest shook his head, spraying twigs everywhere. "Family? No. Just trees. And animal friends."

"Isn't that sad?" Olive said.

"Wait a minute," said her dad, rubbing his chin. "I remember reading about a wild child spotted by some hikers in the forest a few years ago. I wonder if that was you."

Forest thought back and had a vague memory of some noisy hikers.

Olive turned to her father. "See, Dad. He doesn't *have* a family. No place to go. We *have* to take care of him! We have to try to—"

"Are you serious?" Ryan interrupted. "We don't know anything about him. He's wearing mud pants!"

Their dad thought about it. "Come on, Ryan," he said. "He's only a kid, probably the same age as Olive. How much trouble can he be?"

"I know, right?" exclaimed Olive. "And I'll keep an eye on him."

"I think you'll need to keep *more* than just one eye on him," Ryan muttered.

Their dad stuck his hand out to shake the boy's hand. "Welcome to the family, Forest."

Forest looked at the hand and then grabbed it, using it as leverage to swing himself up onto Olive's dad's shoulders. He perched there, grinning proudly.

Olive's dad wasn't sure what to do. He looked at Olive, who shrugged and smiled nervously.

"See how friendly he is?" she said. "He already likes you."

Her dad decided to go with it. "I guess that's how they say hello where he's from?"

Olive looked up at Forest, still on her father's shoulders, now making birdcalls.

"Forest, please come down," Olive asked nicely.

Forest hopped down easily.

"My dad was trying to shake your hand," she explained. "That's how you're supposed to say hello."

Forest looked at his own hand. Then he shook it back and forth. He shook the other one, too, and it soon looked like a dance.

"We'll work on it," Olive said quickly.

They unloaded the car, which Forest thought was a big game. He kept putting everything back in the car until Olive asked him to stop. To Olive's surprise, he did stop as soon as she said the word.

She didn't have to ask a million times or get interrupted, like she did with her brother. She didn't have to fight to be heard. Forest listened to her. He *heard* her.

She realized she liked that. A lot.

Chapter 4

Olive and Forest stood outside the front door of the house. Actually, Olive stood and Forest crouched, trying to communicate with a snail on the ground. Olive looked at Forest's skin, which was still covered with dirt and muck, and realized she couldn't let him in the house like that.

"Okay, Forest, we need to get you cleaned up," she said.

For a second, Olive thought about

having Forest take a regular shower, but then she thought he was too dirty to go *through* the house to get to the shower. She spied the hose coiled next to the house.

Why not? she thought. *Water is water.*

She led Forest over to the hose and then turned on the water. It was a little cold, but Forest didn't seem to mind. She washed Forest's hands and feet. Olive was just thinking it was going better than expected when suddenly Forest cried, "My turn!" He grabbed the hose from her and sprayed it around, barely missing Olive.

"Er, no, Forest. . . . That's not how you . . . ," she began.

Forest held the hose above his head, letting the water pour down his face.

"Oh, that's better!" she cried happily.

He tried to stick it up his nose. *Never mind.* After quickly realizing that *that* wasn't a good idea, he splashed around, stomping his feet, looking like he was having a good time. Olive kind of wished she could join in. . . . She shook her head to clear away that thought and refocused on her task.

Forest was mostly clean! A layer of dirt had washed away. Olive had to admit

it was an *unconventional* shower, but at least it had worked. She turned the hose off, and Forest shook himself out like a dog, making his matted hair stand up at crazy angles.

"Forest like showers," he said, water dripping down his face.

He turned to go climb a tree—and get dirty again—when Olive called out. "Stop! Please! Stay there! Let me go get a towel," she said.

While she ran inside, Forest walked over and turned the hose back on. Just then, Ryan came outside to check the mailbox.

"Ryan need shower, too!" said Forest.

"What? No!" yelled Ryan.

When Olive returned with the towel,

Ryan was dripping from head to toe. He snarled at both Forest and Olive and stomped into the house, water dripping behind him.

"Ryan not like showers?" Forest asked.

Olive giggled. "He likes to take them *inside* the house." She wrapped the towel around Forest. "Come on." She led him into the house.

"Whoa . . . ," said Forest. "Whoa. Big tent."

"Oh, I forgot," said Olive. "You've probably never been inside a house before."

"House?" repeated Forest.

Olive nodded. "Yes, this is where we live. This is our house," she explained. "We eat here, sleep here, hang out here."

"Hang out?" said Forest.

"That's right," said Olive. "Let's get you some clothes. Follow me."

Forest slowly followed. Along the way, Olive had to repeat "Don't touch that. Or that. Or that."

Olive ducked into her brother's room and grabbed some of Ryan's old clothes for Forest to wear. She hoped her brother wouldn't notice.

"Here, put these on," she said, hand-ing the clothes to Forest. "Then I can show you around."

Olive led Forest to her room and had him change into the clothes while she waited in the hall. A few minutes later, he emerged—clothes inside out, but Olive didn't think it was worth fixing. Instead, she thought she should deal with the next hurdle: Forest's hair. She grabbed a brush and tried to run it through his hair, but the brush immediately snapped in half. That was when she discovered the pinecones and other strange things lodged in there.

"Hmm . . . perhaps we'll leave your hair alone for now," said Olive.

"Okay," said Forest, not really listening. He wanted to explore the house!

Olive gave him the grand tour of the upstairs and then led him down to the kitchen, with its sunny yellow walls, and into the living room, where she sat on the comfy brown couch. In front of it was a coffee table, and a big chandelier hung from above. On each side of the couch were bookcases crammed with books.

Forest bounced up and down on the couch, unable to sit still.

"Living room fun!" he exclaimed.

Olive laughed. "Yes, living room fun."

He was bouncing for only a minute before curiosity took over. He raced around the room. "What's this? And this?" he asked repeatedly, picking up random objects. He had never seen a coaster or a

book or even a lamp. He loved when Olive showed him how to click it on and off.

Then Forest saw a large black thing in the corner. He moved toward it, not sure what it was. Suddenly it came to life! Forest spun around and saw Olive holding a thin, rectangular device. He looked worried.

"It's okay," she told him. "It's just the remote for the television." She pointed to

the big screen. "That's a TV. We watch it for fun."

Forest looked back at the TV. On-screen, a cartoon was playing. Two evil raccoon ninjas were facing off against a small but fierce opossum.

Fascinated, Forest leaned in to watch the battle. It was not going well for the opossum.

"Run, opossum!" yelled Forest. "Run!" The evil raccoon ninjas had gained the upper hand. They cornered the opossum and slowly advanced on him. Forest couldn't just stand by. "I'll save you!" he cried.

He leaped forward and punched the raccoons as hard as he could.

Crack!

Chapter 5

Olive ran to Forest and examined his hand.

"Ouch," said Forest, looking at the scratches.

"What was that noise?" Ryan called, rushing down the stairs.

And then he saw it: a big crack in the now blank TV screen.

"What did he do?" Ryan barked at Olive.

Olive gulped. "He's never seen car-
toons before! He was trying to save an
opossum! It was actually quite brave, if the
show had . . . you know . . . been real."

"Seriously?" replied Ryan. "That's lame."
Then he looked sadly at his video game
console. "Aw, man. Now I won't be able to
play any of my games. Wait until Dad
hears about this!"

"Hears about what?" said their father,
walking into the living room.

Ryan angrily explained what had happened.

"It sounds like it was an accident," said their father. "Besides, maybe it's not such a bad thing not to have a working TV. More time for reading and family games!"

Ryan growled in frustration.

Forest growled back. He thought it was a game!

Ryan blinked. Forest's growl had sounded like a real animal's.

Ryan snickered. "I hope he doesn't do that to Gam Gam."

At that, Olive and her dad looked at each other, suddenly worried. "Oh no! Gam Gam!"

"Who Gam Gam?" asked Forest.

"Gam Gam is my grandmother," said Olive. "She's super proper and super strict." Olive explained that Gam Gam's real name was Regina Gina Regle. Her back was ramrod straight, her dresses always starched, her hair always pinned back, and her expression always disapproving.

"Olive, you know how Gam Gam can be," said her father. "If you want Forest to stay, you better teach him some manners and how things work in the regular world."

"Okay, Dad," Olive replied, secretly worrying about how she was going to do that.

Her father suddenly looked serious. "And he has to be ready for Gam Gam's birthday dinner."

Olive's eyes widened. "But . . . but . . . that's only twenty-four hours away!"

"I'm sorry, honey," her father said, and left the room.

As soon as he was out of earshot, Ryan turned to his sister. "There's *no way* Gam Gam is going to approve of Forest. I bet she'll persuade Dad to find another home for him."

Olive gasped. That was what had happened to her hamster, Furball. And her lizard, Bubbles. *And* her poor ferret,

Mr. Stripes. Gam Gam never thought they were "proper" pets. But Olive really wanted Forest to stay. She just had to figure out *how* to make that happen.

She turned to explain to Forest about grandmothers, but he had disappeared. She spun around and saw out the window that he was in the backyard. He was happily climbing a tree trunk and swinging on the limbs.

"Olive play, too," Forest called out, and waved.

But Olive wasn't sure. She worried she couldn't climb as well as Forest. Then she squared her shoulders. She would give it a try. If she failed, she had a feeling Forest wouldn't laugh at her like Ryan would. Within a few minutes, Olive relaxed a little and actually enjoyed herself. She watched as Forest talked with the squirrels. He squeaked and chittered at them, and then he chased them around a tree trunk. He helped dislodge a stuck acorn, for which the squirrels seemed very grateful. They discovered a cute white bunny that Olive wanted to play with, but Forest said the rabbit was in a hurry and couldn't stay.

At one point, Forest climbed a tree to

a birdhouse. A pair of birds chirped at him, and in response, Forest gave a high-pitched whistle.

"What are they saying? What are you saying to them?" Olive said as she climbed up and sat next to him on the branch.

"They catch insects and dig for worms," said Forest.

"I wish I could talk to them the way you do," Olive said wistfully.

Forest nodded. "Olive can."

So Olive tried chirping and whistling, but she couldn't whistle very well, and it came out more like a breathy hoot. Apparently she didn't say the right thing, because the birds swooped down and buzzed her head!

"What did I say? What did I say?" cried Olive.

"You said, 'Nest stinks. Bird wiggy wiggy twiggy beak.'" Forest shook his shaggy head. "Birds no joke about beaks. Very serious."

Olive felt bad. Here she was, with someone who could actually talk to animals, and all she did was make them laugh at her and fly away!

To make matters worse, she spotted Ryan watching from his bedroom window.

"How's it going? Is he even human yet?" Ryan called out.

"Mind your own business!" Olive yelled back. She climbed down the tree.

How am I going to have Forest pass the Gam Gam test? She was worried.

"Why Olive look sad?" Forest asked.

"We need to impress Gam Gam so you can stay," Olive said.

"Why?"

"Because she's Dad's mother," explained Olive. "And her opinion matters to him. This is going to be hard because I don't think she likes me. She likes Ryan better."

"Why?" asked Forest. "Olive more fun."

Olive grinned. It was nice to hear that. "Thanks. But Gam Gam doesn't even remember my name. She calls me Alice. Dad says that I shouldn't say anything to her about it. But it's weird!"

Forest nodded in sympathy.

At that moment, they heard a loud *ribbit*! Forest climbed down and within seconds spotted a frog. He gently picked it up, and Olive smiled with glee. She had never seen or touched a frog before, only heard them in the backyard.

"Ryan's scared of frogs," Olive said.

"Why?" asked Forest.

"Once when we were at Gam Gam's," said Olive, "Ryan fell in the pond and a frog jumped on his head. But this is one cool frog! Let's go show my dad."

Olive led Forest back to the house and opened the screen door. They found her dad in the kitchen.

"Look, Dad!" said Olive. "We found a frog in the backyard!"

Olive's dad was busy stirring a bubbling pot of tomato sauce. He turned from the stove, wearing an apron that read WORLD'S WORST COOK, WORLD'S BEST DAD. "Whoa, cool," he said. "But let's keep it out of the kitchen, okay? We don't want it to end up as dinner!"

Olive and Forest *both* looked horrified.

"Relax! I'm just kidding!" said Dad.

Olive laughed. "Whew!"

But Forest still looked worried. His eyes darted back and forth between the simmering pot and the frog. He wanted to

get the frog outside as soon as possible.
He turned and ran—smack into the screen
door.

"Oof!" said Forest.

"*Ribbit!*" croaked the frog as it leaped

out of Forest's hands, hopped into the
living room and onto the coffee table.

"Catch it!" yelled Olive.

The frog hopped from the coffee table
to the top of one of the bookshelves.
Bailey, sensing commotion, ran into the
room and started barking.

"I got it! I got it!" said Olive, climbing
onto the sofa.

Before she could grab it, the frog
leaped onto the chandelier. Forest followed suit, grabbing onto the chandelier

with his right hand and trying to grab the frog with his left. His legs dangled as he and the chandelier swung back and forth.

"Come down, Forest!" yelled Olive. "You can't do that!"

"Forest! Stop! You'll break it!" called her dad.

Bailey ran in circles, barking wildly and sniffing around.

Forest stretched out his arm. He nearly reached the frog when . . .

RIBBIT!

The frog made a flying leap and landed right on top of Olive's dad's head. He tried to grab the frog but only managed to whack himself in the face with a wooden spoon he'd forgotten he was holding.

"Ow!" he exclaimed.

Olive's dad fell down, and the frog leaped back into the kitchen. Forest dropped from the chandelier and chased the frog, jumping over Olive's father, who was slightly dazed. Olive and Bailey followed, both of them jumping over him, too.

"Sorry, Dad!" Olive yelled behind her.

In the kitchen, the panicking frog leaped onto the counter. It hopped up to the top of the refrigerator and then down to the sink, which was, unfortunately, filled with dirty dishes. As it took its next leap, milk and cereal splattered everywhere.

"Oh no!" cried Olive.

"Get it before it breaks anything in here!" yelled her dad.

Olive and her dad bounded after the frog, but that seemed to make the creature jump faster. It hopped up onto the counter, where her dad had placed the spices for the tomato sauce.

"Shh! We have to be quiet or we'll scare him," Olive said to her father.

She slowly tiptoed up to the frog, hoping to grab it. She nearly had it when . . . Forest leaped up onto the counter! Salt and oregano and black pepper flew everywhere.

"Achoo! Achoo! ACHOO!" they all sneezed.

That last big sneeze belonged to Olive's father, and he accidentally knocked into a stack of clean dishes.

"Look out!" he cried.

The dishes fell to the floor with a *crash*!

Luckily no one got hurt, but the frog escaped. Olive watched as the frog hopped out of the kitchen and up the stairs. She turned to survey the damage.

Suddenly they heard Ryan's voice. "Aahhh! Why is there a *frog* in my *bed*?"

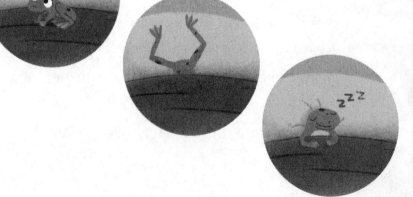

Chapter 6

Olive, her father, and Forest all ran up the stairs to Ryan's bedroom.

"Calm down," their dad told Ryan as they entered.

"Calm down? *Calm down?*" repeated Ryan, his voice rising. "There is a frog in my bed! Why is there a frog in my bed?"

Olive started to explain. "We wanted

to show Dad the frog we found in the backyard, but then things kind of got out of control."

"Well, obviously," Ryan said snottily. "Forest needs to keep his 'friends' outside!"

"Because Ryan scared of frogs?" Forest asked innocently.

Olive began to laugh, but a stern look from her father stopped her.

"*Some* things don't belong inside!" Ryan said angrily.

Forest looked around. "Uh . . . Where froggy?" he asked, his brows furrowed.

They all looked back at the bed, but the frog wasn't there.

"Oh my gosh! It's loose again!" Ryan exclaimed. "How am I supposed to sleep with a frog loose in the house?"

"Ryan, take it easy," said his father. "I'm sure we'll find it."

An hour later, they hadn't found the frog *anywhere* in the house. Olive's dad was confident that the frog would turn up. In the kitchen, he and Olive surveyed the broken dishes and spilled food and started to clean it all up.

"I'm sorry about dinner," Olive said softly.

"It's okay," said her father.

"Forest make dinner!" said Forest.

Before Olive or her father could protest, Forest ran outside. He returned with a colorful collection of items. Olive recognized *some* of them, like the red berries that grew on the bush in the backyard. But she was a bit suspicious of what

looked like a leaf sandwich with brown stuff in the middle.

"You eat that?" said Ryan.

Suddenly the sandwich moved!

"Yikes!" screamed Olive.

A slimy worm climbed out from between the leaves and crawled up Forest's arm.

Olive's mouth dropped open. "You eat worms, Forest?"

Forest shook his head. "Forest no like. Worms give bad bellyache. Must be in there by accident."

Forest took the lowly worm and put him back outside. When he returned, still holding his "dinner" suggestion, Olive's father came to the rescue.

"That's really nice of you to offer to

make dinner, but how about we just order some pizza?" he suggested. "We can try that . . . uh . . . sandwich some other time."

Forest seemed fine with that, while Olive and Ryan breathed a sigh of relief.

Later, after their bellies were full of pizza, Forest was still full of energy. He darted through the house, picking up various objects and asking what they were, as he had done earlier in the day.

Olive followed behind, answering him. At first she found it fun as she explained what a salt shaker was for or what a chessboard was for. But after two hours of that, Olive was tired. She was even relieved when her father said it was time for bed.

"Olive, here's a new toothbrush for Forest," her dad said. "Can you take him upstairs and show him how to brush his teeth?"

"Sure, Dad," said Olive.

"Not that he needs it," said her dad. "His teeth are pearly white."

Forest smiled widely.

"Oh. You're right," said Olive. "How . . . ?"

Her dad smiled. "He probably hasn't had any sugar in years. Or ever."

"Come on, Forest," said Olive. "Unless you want a lecture on healthy eating."

"Do I?" asked Forest.

"No. Definitely *not*," said Olive.

In the bathroom, Olive grabbed her own toothbrush and squeezed a pea-sized amount of toothpaste onto it. She motioned for Forest to do the same.

Unfortunately he squeezed too hard and a wriggly stream of toothpaste squirted out.

"Whoa!" exclaimed Olive. "Just a little bit on the toothbrush!"

Forest stared at his toothbrush. "Look!" he said earnestly. "Only little here."

He was right. There *was* only a little on the toothbrush—because all the rest was everywhere else! Long strips of blue toothpaste covered the mirror and the sink. Forest tried to wipe them off, but that just smeared the sticky stuff.

"I'm too tired to clean another room tonight," said Olive. "Let's just deal with it tomorrow."

"Okay."

"You might want to wash the tooth-paste off your face, though."

"Okay," said Forest. "I go get hose."

"No, no, no," said Olive. "Do it in the sink. Wash your face in the sink."

"Okay." Forest reached for what he thought was the sink.

"That's not the sink!"

"But it big bowl of clean water."

"*This* is the sink," said Olive. "Over here. This is a faucet. Water comes out. Like this."

"Then what is big bowl of clean water for?" asked Forest.

Olive told him.

Forest looked shocked. "You do not go outside?"

"No! Gross. Look, it flushes. See?" She flushed.

Forest needed to see the toilet flush only several dozen more times before Olive could pry his attention back to the sink.

"Okay," she said. "Now clean yourself up while I get you a towel. I'll be right back."

Thirty seconds later, Olive returned to the bathroom to see that Forest had *completely* covered himself in blue toothpaste!

He looked at Olive, a proud grin across his face. "Toothpaste get you clean, right? So Forest use everywhere! Now Forest all clean!"

"I . . . uh . . . Toothpaste is just for teeth!" Olive sputtered.

"Ohhh," said Forest. "So should not have cleaned everywhere with this?" He held up Olive's toothbrush.

She sighed. "Just get the toothpaste off, please. With water. From the sink! I'm going to get myself a new toothbrush."

After Forest had splashed about a gallon of water everywhere in the bathroom *except* his face, an exhausted Olive said, "Time for bed. You can sleep in my room. Let's get a bed made up for you. I'm going to get some sheets and a blanket."

When Olive returned to her room with the linens to make a bed on the floor, she couldn't find Forest anywhere. But she could hear him snoring.

"Forest?" she called softly.

He wasn't on the floor or on her bed. Olive looked under her bed, but no luck. Then she spotted him on top of her white bookshelf. He was lying on a pile of feathers that reminded her of a nest. Olive spun around and saw what was left of her feather pillow, now all torn up. Olive wasn't even mad. She realized that Forest was probably used to sleeping up in a tree, so why not up on a bookshelf?

With a yawn, Olive decided it was time she turned in, too. She crawled into bed and fell asleep instantly.

Chapter 7

The next morning, when Olive woke, she rubbed her eyes and stretched.

"Good morning, Forest," she said.

But Forest didn't answer.

Olive quickly jumped out of bed and went to inspect Forest's nest on top of the bookcase. But there was no Forest, just feathers slowly drifting down to the floor.

"Oh no," she worried aloud. "I hope

nothing happened to him." Then she had a very sad thought: *I hope he didn't leave!*

As she threw open the door, she grabbed her robe, putting it on as she called out, "Forest? Forest!"

Crash!

Olive gasped and hurried down the stairs. At the bottom of the staircase, she saw a hole in the window behind the couch. Olive cocked her head to one side and realized the hole was very much shaped like a football. She ran to the window and peered outside. On the patio sat a football surrounded by glass pieces. She whirled around and saw Ryan standing there, with Forest next to him.

"I was trying to teach Forest how to play football," said Ryan, a sly smile on his face.

"*In the house?*" yelled Olive.

Ryan tried to look innocent. He didn't really succeed. Olive knew he was being a jerk on purpose.

"What?" Ryan said with a shrug. "I didn't want to have to put on shoes."

But Olive knew something else was going on. "This is just because you're mad about the frog in your bed and—"

As usual, Ryan cut her off. "I don't know what you're talking about. Like I said, I was just teaching Forest some football moves."

Just then, Forest piped up. "Why called foot-ball when you don't use your foot? And ball shaped like egg. Should be called hand-egg, not foot-ball."

"Good point, Forest," said Olive. Then she turned to her brother. "Ryan,

you *know* it's not okay to throw the hand-egg—I mean, football—in the house!"

"You can't prove a thing," said Ryan. Then he got close to her and whispered in her ear. "I can't wait to see what he does when Gam Gam is here. Maybe that will convince Dad that keeping Forest around is a bad idea."

Olive couldn't believe her ears. "Ryan!"

"I'm sure you guys can take care of this mess before Dad wakes up," he said, striding upstairs. "I've got things to do, *Alice*."

Olive fumed. It was bad enough when Gam Gam called her Alice. But hearing that name come out of Ryan's mouth made her brain bubble with rage. She watched her brother walk upstairs, and with each step he took, she got angrier and angrier.

She turned to Forest. "How could Ryan do this to me?" she said. "He knows he's not supposed to play ball in the house. And Gam Gam will be here *tonight*!"

"Uh . . . ," began Forest.

"And even though I didn't break that window, I'm responsible for you, like Dad

said, so I'd better figure something out,"
she said, now pacing the room. "How dare
he call me Alice! I hate it when Gam Gam
calls me that, and he knows that!"

"I, uh—" said Forest.

Olive interrupted. "I'm not going to let
him win. I'm not going to let him *or* Gam
Gam say you have to go away!"

"Okay . . . ," started Forest.

"Well, I'm glad we've had this little talk, Forest," said Olive with a deep sigh of relief.

"Uh . . . me too?" said Forest.

"Now, let's see what we can do about that window," said Olive, marching off to inspect it.

After cleaning up the shattered glass with a dustpan and broom, Olive decided that the only thing they could do for now was cover up the hole. Forest had some interesting suggestions on what they could use: a leaf, the dog, and his butt.

Olive laughed. "Interesting ideas, Forest, but I have another suggestion."

Inside, Olive grabbed some blank paper and her favorite markers scented with fruity smells. But when Forest tried to eat one, she traded them for regular markers.

"Let's draw pictures to cover up the hole," said Olive.

"Okay," agreed Forest.

Olive drew a picture of her and her father at the park. When she looked at

Forest's picture, it was of him and some really big hairy feet attached to really big hairy legs attached to—well, she wasn't sure because Forest ran out of paper to draw on.

With some tape, Olive put the drawings up over the hole. She cocked her head to the side. "I think it'll work," she said.

"You think *what* will work?" said her father's voice behind them.

Olive froze. How was she going to tell him about the hole in the window? She slowly turned around and saw him standing there in his bathrobe and slippers. "Hi, Dad!" she said, a little too cheerfully.

"Hiiiii . . . ," said her father suspiciously.

"We were just doing a little decorating for Gam Gam's party tonight," Olive

said quickly, trying to steer her dad away from the window.

"Oh, good thinking," said her father. "How about I get out some streamers to hang, too?"

"Good idea, Dad," said Olive as she watched her father head to the hall closet.

"Whew!" she whispered to Forest. "That was a close one!"

"A close what?" said Forest. He looked around. "Was something close to us?"

"I'll explain it to you later," said Olive. "Right now, we have to try to cram in everything else I need to teach you about good manners before Gam Gam gets here! She is super-duper proper!"

"Uh-oh," said Forest.

She sat him down at the dining room table. "Okay," said Olive. "Table manners are really important to Gam Gam, so you need to sit still. She hates it when I get all squirmy in my seat."

"Squirmy?" asked Forest.

"Here, I'll show you," said Olive. She plopped down in the chair next to his and then sat completely straight and without moving.

When Forest tried that, he lasted about 1.2 seconds. Then he wiggled his nose. Then his toes. Then his fingers. Finally, he jumped up on the chair and declared, "Manners dumb!"

Olive nodded. "They're not my favorite thing, either, but we have to do them. Let's move on to something else."

"Ugh," said Forest. "How many manners are there?"

Olive shrugged. "Sometimes it feels like there're a million. Some of them I don't really understand. Like, why can't you put your elbows on the table?"

Forest put *his* elbows on the table. "I can. You can't?"

Olive just smiled, realizing it wasn't worth explaining that one to Forest.

Instead she went into the kitchen and pulled some leftover mac and cheese out of the refrigerator. She placed the dish in front of Forest, with a fork on the side. "This is called mac and—what are you doing?"

"Eating," said Forest, happily holding the cheesy glop in both hands and cramming it into his mouth.

"No!" said Olive. "Not with your hands! Use a fork!"

"What is fork?"

"This!" she said, pointing.

"Oh," said Forest, picking it up. He

used it to scratch an itch on his back. "You sure for eating? We didn't eat pizza with it."

Olive sighed. *This is harder than I thought it was going to be!*

For the next hour and a half, Olive taught Forest how to say "please" and "thank you," how to use a napkin (and not as a hat), how to pass a dish (and not throw it), how grooming someone's hair for bugs is not appropriate, and how burping is not something to do in someone's ear (or at all).

As the afternoon wore on, Forest got tired and began confusing his *pleases* with his *thank yous* and which parts of his body he was allowed to scratch.

Olive finally stopped. She'd taught

him as many manners as she could, and he seemed to remember most of them, most of the time.

But would it be enough to pass the Gam Gam test?

Chapter 8

At 6:00 p.m. precisely, the doorbell rang. Gam Gam was always exactly on time.

Olive's dad opened the door for his mother. "Happy birthday!" he said to her. He kissed her on the cheek.

"Mind the hair," Gam Gam said. She had silver hair piled on top of her head, with not a single strand out of place. It often reminded Olive of a beehive.

"Happy birthday!" said Olive as Gam Gam came inside.

"Thank you, Alice," said Gam Gam.

Olive sighed. She desperately wanted to say something about her name, but she kept quiet instead. Just like always.

"Where's Forest?" Olive's father asked.

"He's still getting ready," she replied. "He said he wanted to be fancy. Ryan told him he'd lend him something to wear."

"Uh-oh," said her father.

Just then, Forest bounded down the stairs. He wore a towel as a cape, no shirt, and a tie around his head.

"Oh no!" Olive whispered.

Forest ran up to Gam Gam, and the sight of him caused her to recoil. Then

Forest remembered what he was taught. "Nice to smell you!"

"*Meet* you! Nice to *meet* you!" Olive said, trying to help.

"Oh!" said Forest. "Nice to meet you." He held out his hands and shook them around.

Gam Gam took a step back. "Who on earth is this?"

"This is Forest, Mom," Olive's dad said. "Remember, I told you about him on the phone?"

"I assumed you were joking," Gam Gam replied with a haughty sniff.

"Not at all," replied Olive's dad. "He's only been with us for one day, and Olive has already done a great job trying to teach Forest how things work around here."

"Not great enough," mumbled Ryan.

"Ryan, do you have something you want to share?" asked his father, annoyed.

"No," replied Ryan, tightening his jaw.

Olive was glad to hear her father was proud of her. Now she and Forest had to convince Gam Gam that Forest should become a permanent member of the family.

A few minutes later, they sat down to dinner. Olive was stuck sitting next to Gam Gam.

"Oh, my favorite!" said Gam Gam, seeing the meal of baked ham and boiled brussels sprouts. She picked up the bowl of vegetables and put some on her plate. Then she served some to Olive.

"Uh, I don't really like—" began Olive in a soft voice.

But Gam Gam cut her off. "Of course you do. Everyone likes boiled brussels sprouts."

"No, really, I—"

Gam Gam didn't seem to hear her. Olive felt like her grandmother never listened to her. Olive stared at the vegetables, wishing they'd just roll off her plate.

"I *love* brussels sprouts!" said Ryan.

"That's my boy," said Gam Gam

approvingly. Ryan then snatched the brussels sprouts off his plate when Gam Gam turned away and fed them to Bailey.

Olive rolled her eyes. Her brother was so annoying.

"Dad, can you please pass the rolls?" Olive asked, nice and loud, hoping Gam Gam would appreciate her good manners.

But it backfired.

"Don't fill up on bread, young lady," Gam Gam declared.

"I wasn't going to. I was—" began Olive.

"I should hope not," said Gam Gam.

Olive sighed, feeling deflated. She wished Gam Gam would let her talk. Olive felt like she couldn't say what she wanted to around her grandmother.

Throughout dinner, Olive kept a close eye on Forest. Unfortunately Forest sat right across from Gam Gam, squatting on his seat with his knees up by his ears—kind of like a frog.

"Sit down like a proper boy," Gam Gam instructed. "And no squirming!"

Olive piped up. "Well, he's new to this and—"

"Quiet, young lady," said Gam Gam. "And eat your vegetables."

"Okay," Olive said timidly.

Meanwhile, Forest actually really liked the brussels sprouts, but he chewed loudly and with his mouth open. Most of his food stayed inside, but not all. He used his napkin to wipe his mouth, and then put it on his head. Olive cringed.

Gam Gam recoiled. "Have you not taught that boy *any* manners?" she asked, outraged.

"Yes, we have!" said Olive. "He used his napkin!"

"Yeah, you should have seen him before," Ryan said with a laugh.

Ryan got an annoyed look from his father.

"Hey, Forest," said Ryan. "I'm sure Gam Gam would love to meet your 'friends' after dinner."

"How about now?" said Forest. Then

he gave one long whistle and a series of short chirps.

"What is he doing?" said Gam Gam, looking horrified. "One does not *whistle* at the table!"

Chirp! Whistle!

"I said, no whistling at the table—"

"That's coming from *outside*, Gam Gam," said Olive. "Look!"

Dozens of birds flocked outside the windows. Robins, sparrows, starlings, even a crow or two. They tweeted, chirped, twittered, and cawed.

One clever crow poked its beak through the covered-up hole in the window, tearing right through the drawings Olive had put up. Suddenly dozens of birds burst through the hole and flew around the room, squawking and flapping.

They tore at the streamers that had been hung for the party.

Behind them, squirrels and a rabbit scampered in.

"Hello, friends!" said Forest, jumping onto his chair and waving his arms.

Olive's mouth dropped open in horror. Ryan's face beamed with nasty delight.

Her dad bolted out of his chair, grabbed a broom, and tried to shoo the animals back out the window, but it didn't work. Critters kept coming in.

"Where did that hole come from?" exclaimed Olive's dad, pointing at the window. Then he looked sternly at Olive and Ryan.

"Uh . . . ," started Ryan.

But before Ryan could say anything else, Forest hopped in front of their dad.

"Forest make hole," said Forest. He dropped his head. "Sorry."

Ryan's mouth dropped open in shock—he could not believe that Forest had covered for him. He started to feel a tiny bit bad for trying to get Forest in trouble.

Meanwhile, Bailey was in doggy heaven, barking and chasing after the animals.

The creatures scattered, squawked, and screeched.

"Get these wretched beasts *off* me!" yelled Gam Gam.

The others turned to see a pair of red-bellied robins building a new nest—right on top of Gam Gam's hair!

Gam Gam waved her hands around wildly, trying to get rid of the birds. She screamed as a rabbit nibbled at a brussels

sprout on her plate. Olive watched in horror as the *same* frog they couldn't find yesterday hopped right onto Gam Gam's head.

"Aaaaah!" Gam Gam shrieked.

The frog flicked its tongue out, nabbed a fly, and began to messily eat it.

As Gam Gam screamed, Forest said, "Froggy!" and lunged toward Gam Gam.

The force caused Gam Gam to fall backward in her chair.

"Gam Gam!" Olive yelled.

"Mom!" said Olive's dad.

"Get me up *now*!" thundered Gam Gam.

Olive and her father helped her up. Standing there, with her hair a complete mess and her outfit disheveled, Gam Gam looked a lot less scary to Olive. Until she spoke . . .

"That . . . that . . . *wild child* must go!" Gam Gam demanded. "Right this minute!"

Chapter 9

"*No!*" said Olive.

Gam Gam turned to her. "*What* did you say, young lady?"

"I will not let Forest go!" said Olive. In that moment, she realized that if Forest could be himself, then Olive could, too, and she could stand up for herself. Next to Gam Gam, both Ryan and their dad stood openmouthed. They had never seen Olive say no to Gam Gam before.

"He *must* go, Alice!" insisted Gam Gam.

"Okay, everyone, calm down," said Olive's dad, locking the screen door after finally herding most of the creatures back outside. "I'm sure there's a—"

"Forest is my *friend*," said Olive. "I don't get rid of friends. Although he may be different, that doesn't make him bad."

At that, Forest joined Olive, putting an arm around her. Then he spoke. "This Olive. Not Alice. *Olive.*"

Olive gasped. And then she froze. She wasn't sure what to do next.

Well, she thought, *it's now or never.*

"Forest is right," she said to Gam Gam. "At least the *wild child* can remember my name! You're my own grandmother and you can't even be bothered to learn my name!"

Gam Gam looked shocked, and then she softened. "But I *do* know who you are. In fact, I always tell my weekly bridge group that I'm so proud of my grand-daughter."

"Then why do you always call me Alice?" said Olive, exasperated.

Gam Gam's hand flew to her mouth.

"Oh dear. I didn't realize I was doing that. Let me explain." She motioned for Olive to join her on the couch. They brushed aside some lingering squirrels and a blue jay. "Alice was the name of my sister, who was one of my favorite people in the whole world."

"Really?" Olive asked.

"Yes," replied Gam Gam. "You look a lot like she did when we were little, and I really miss her." She looked at Forest, who was perched on the arm of the couch. "I was surprised by this wild boy, but then again, Alice did have a wild streak in her, too. And a good heart, just like you, Olive."

Touched, Olive hugged Gam Gam, keeping it to herself that her grandmother now smelled like a stinky petting zoo.

As a show of support for Forest, Gam Gam removed the scarf from around her neck. She tied it around her forehead to copy him. Olive grinned widely. Then Forest jumped down and stuck out his hand to Gam Gam. She took it, and they shook hands correctly, even though Forest was unclear on when to stop shaking hands.

"Welcome to the family, young man," Gam Gam said.

At that, Olive hugged Gam Gam again, and then Forest threw his arms around both of them.

After they finished dinner and enjoyed birthday cake for dessert, it was time for Gam Gam to head home.

Olive was surprised to discover she

was actually sad that Gam Gam was leaving. For her, it was the best time she had ever had with her grandmother.

"Thank you for a most memorable birthday," Gam Gam said.

"You're welcome," said Olive. "Maybe next time you can tell me more about Alice?"

Gam Gam smiled and nodded.

Olive felt a bolt of confidence. She had done it—really done it! It had been super stressful, but she had gotten Forest ready to meet Gam Gam *and* she'd stood her ground.

She breathed a teeny-tiny sigh of relief.

Gam Gam was halfway down the walkway outside when she turned around. "Oh, Olive, good luck with Forest at school next week!"

Olive froze. *"School?"*

She looked over at Forest, who was on his hands and knees having a growling competition with Bailey. Forest was winning. Olive's eyes grew big. She imagined Forest at school, jumping from desk to desk and causing plenty of chaos.

Forest at school? she thought. *Uh-oh!!!*

About the Author

Tara Zann can't imagine living in a place without tall trees. Just like Forest, she has a spirit of adventure, though she might use a zip line instead of swinging from tree to tree on a long, dangling vine. She has no official pets, but dozens of creatures tend to stop by her backyard tree house on a regular basis.

Read ALL the books in the WILD CHILD series!

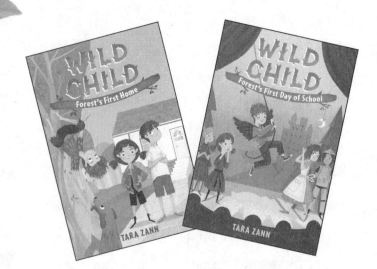

Read a sneak peek of the next book: Forest's First Day of School!

Looking unsure but following Mrs. Finn's encouragement, Forest walked slowly to the front of the class. Mrs. Finn signaled that he should turn around to face the class. Forest looked at Mrs. Finn with a look that said, *Now what do I do?*

"Why don't you tell us a little about yourself?" suggested Mrs. Finn.

"Uh . . ." said Forest.

He looked over the sea of unfamiliar

faces. He'd never been looked at by so many people at once. He didn't want to disappoint Olive, but Forest had absolutely no idea what he was supposed to say!

Mrs. Finn could tell that Forest was uncomfortable, so she tried something different. "Forest, why don't you tell us something you like or like doing?"

Forest thought for a moment. Then his eye caught something across the room— the hamster.

"Forest like animals," he said proudly. "Forest talk to animals."

"Oh, really?" said Mrs. Finn, thinking Forest was just playing.

"Yes," insisted Forest. "The hamster over there wants a bigger cage with a wheel and a fountain and . . . what is a 'piano'?"

Mrs. Finn laughed uncomfortably. "Well, you certainly have quite an imagination, Forest! I'm sure that Henrietta the Hamster is perfectly happy in her current home."

"Oh, no," said Forest. "Henrietta is boy hamster! His real name is," Forest made a little squeaking sound.